The Diamond Princess and the Magic Ball

THE JEWEL KINGDOM

The Diamond Princess and the Magic Ball

JAHNNA N. MALCOLM

Illustrations by Neal McPheeters

SCHOLASTIC INC.
NEW YORK   TORONTO   LONDON   AUCKLAND   SYDNEY

For Leslie and Lynn,
and their young wizards,
Spencer and Ian

No part of this publication may be reproduced in whole or in part, or stored in a retrieval system, or transmitted in any form or by any means, electronic, mechanical, photocopying, recording, or otherwise, without written permission of the publisher. For information regarding permission, write to Scholastic Inc., Attention: Permissions Department, 555 Broadway, New York, NY 10012.

ISBN 0-590-11739-4

Text copyright © 1998 by Jahnna Beecham and Malcolm Hillgartner.
Illustrations copyright © 1998 by Scholastic Inc.
All rights reserved. Published by Scholastic Inc.
SCHOLASTIC, LITTLE APPLE PAPERBACKS, and logos are trademarks and/or registered trademarks of Scholastic Inc.

12 11 10 9 8 7 6 5 4 3 2 1   8 9/9 0 1 2 3/0

Printed in the U.S.A.   40
First Scholastic printing, June 1998

CONTENTS

The Diamond Princess and the Magic Ball

THE JEWEL KINGDOM

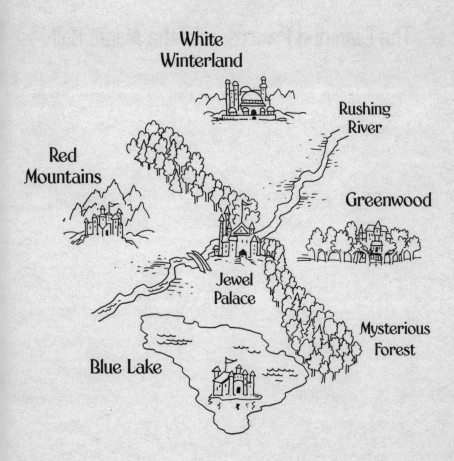

White
Winterland

Rushing
River

Red
Mountains

Greenwood

Jewel
Palace

Mysterious
Forest

Blue Lake

Demetra Meets a Fortune-teller

"Finley, do you think I'm a good princess?" Demetra asked the little fox who sat in the sleigh beside her.

"Of course you're a good princess," Finley replied. "Why do you ask?"

The Diamond Princess was returning from a party at her parents' palace, in the center of the Jewel Kingdom. Queen Jemma and King Regal had invited their four daughters for dinner. During the party Demetra's sisters told wonderful stories about their new lives in their lands.

"Each one of my sisters has done something special for her people," Demetra explained as she retied the silver ribbon around her long brown braid. "But I haven't done anything."

Demetra had three sisters. When they were crowned Jewel Princesses, their parents had given each one of them a land to rule.

Princess Demetra ruled the White Winterland. Her people lived in crystal caves and cottages carved into the snow-covered mountains. They traveled on skis, skates, and sleighs like the one Demetra was driving.

Princess Roxanne was crowned the

Ruby Princess. She lived in her palace in the Red Mountains. Sabrina, the Sapphire Princess, ruled the Blue Lake. Emily, the Emerald Princess, was the youngest of the four sisters. She was given the Greenwood.

"What have your sisters done?" Finley asked. The white fox was Demetra's best friend. He was always there to listen to her troubles.

"Princess Sabrina put a waterwheel on Blue Lake."

Finley nodded. "Oh, yes. I heard it was a great success with the Water Sprites."

"And the Ruby Princess made a special day just for the children of the Red Mountains. They played games, and Hapgood the Dragon gave them rides on his back."

"That must have been fun," Finley said.

Demetra slumped down in her sleigh. "Even Emily made special gift baskets for every creature in the Greenwood."

"What would you like to do?" Finley asked the princess.

"Sometimes I think it would be nice to make a place that was warm and sunny." Demetra sat up excitedly. "We could build a crystal dome. Inside, it would be warm and we could go swimming, instead of skating or skiing. We could skip through the grass and pick flowers."

"That sounds like something *you* would like more than your people would," Finley said as the sleigh whooshed along the border of the White Winterland. "The people of the White Winterland are used to the ice. They love the snow. It's all they've ever known."

Demetra wrapped her white velvet cape around her and whispered, "Sometimes, Finley, I get tired of the snow. Then I pretend our whole land is green. Is that terrible of me?"

Finley patted her hand with his paw. "Of course not, my lady."

Rolf the reindeer was pulling the crystal sleigh. Suddenly he called over his shoulder, "Excuse me, Princess. Something is blocking the road ahead."

Demetra sat forward. At the foot of the hill was a wagon. It was painted blue, with yellow moons and stars. Orange-haired girls in brightly colored dresses danced on a stage in front of the wagon. A crowd of travelers had gathered to watch them.

Finley hopped onto Rolf's back to get a closer look. "Those are Whirligans," he announced. "It looks like they're putting on a show."

"Let's stop and watch!" Demetra's blue eyes twinkled with excitement.

"That's not a good idea," Finley said. "Their wagon is practically touching the Mysterious Forest."

The Mysterious Forest was a dark strip of trees that cut across the Jewel Kingdom. King Regal had warned his daughters to stay away from it. Bad things happened there.

Finley tapped the reindeer on the shoulder. "Try to go around them, Rolf."

"No!" Demetra pulled back on Rolf's reins.

Rolf stopped instantly. Finley rolled off the reindeer's back onto the ground.

"Yeow!" Finley cried, shaking his paw. "That hurt."

Demetra hopped off the sleigh. "Sorry, Finley. I didn't mean to make you fall. But I don't want to miss the show."

"I still don't think this is a good idea," Finley warned.

"Stop worrying," Demetra called over her shoulder. "And come have a little fun."

Finley folded his paws across his chest. "I'm going to stay here with Rolf and guard the sleigh."

"Suit yourself," Demetra replied as she skipped off.

By the time the Diamond Princess reached the wagon, a woman with a gold turban and hoop earrings was on the stage. Her dress was made of yellow and red scarves. Fuzzy purple hair stuck out from under her turban.

"Greetings!" the woman called to the crowd. "I am Madame Zara. I am a fortune-teller. Who would like to have her fortune told?"

Princess Demetra raised her hand. "I would," she sang out. "Please, pick me."

A smile crossed Madame Zara's lips. "Come and join me on the stage."

A huge Whirligan appeared at Demetra's side and lifted her onto the wooden platform.

Madame Zara closed her eyes. "I see we have a princess with us today. Princess Demetra, the Diamond Princess of the White Winterland."

Demetra looked at the crowd and blushed. "Yes, that's me."

"Even I could have guessed that," a boy called from the back of the crowd. "She's

wearing a crown with her diamond jewel on it. Some fortune-teller you are."

Madame Zara's eyes flashed open. She spun around and faced the young boy. "You! Come here!"

Before the boy could say no, two bearded Whirligans grabbed him by the arms and shoved him onto the stage.

The boy wore a green tunic with a rope belt and brown leggings. He had shaggy yellow hair and large brown eyes. He was a little taller than Demetra, but about the same age.

"Your name, boy?" Madame Zara demanded. "What is it?"

The boy looked her in the eye. "You tell me!"

The fortune-teller shook one finger at him. "Don't test me. Zara does not like to be tested."

Demetra took the boy's side. "If you really are a fortune-teller, you should be able to guess his name."

Zara spun to look at the princess. "Zara never *guesses* anything. I *know* that this boy's name is Wink. I also *know* that Wink wanted to be a wizard, but he wasn't good enough. Gallivant sent him home."

"The great Wizard Gallivant?" Demetra gasped. "You know him?"

Wink nodded.

Demetra pointed to her crown. "Gallivant gave me my diamond and made me a Jewel Princess."

Wink still didn't say a word.

"What's the matter?" Madame Zara nudged Wink's shoulder. "Cat got your tongue?"

"I was trying to figure out how you

guessed all those things about me," Wink replied. "And now I know."

The boy pointed to the knapsack slung over his shoulder. A blue robe peeked out from the sack. The boy's name was sewn on the sleeve. "You saw my wizard's robe. And you read my name."

Madame Zara smiled. "But I didn't see your poor dog. The one you have hidden under your shirt."

"You have a dog in there?" Demetra asked. She stared at the boy's green tunic. It was hard to imagine a dog, even the smallest kind, hiding under that shirt.

Now it was Wink's turn to blush. "It isn't exactly a dog," he mumbled. "At least, not right now."

Madame Zara laughed. "Because this little wizard made a big mistake, and turned his dog into a frog."

Just then a tiny green head popped out of Wink's shirt. The frog hopped onto the boy's shoulder and licked his cheek.

"This is my dog, Trumpet," Wink said, embarrassed.

The frog looked at Demetra and, in a big, deep voice said, "Woof!"

Wink the Wizard

Princess Demetra was thrilled. Madame Zara really was a fortune-teller!

Zara knew that Wink was a failed wizard. She even knew that Wink had turned his poor little dog into a frog.

"Oh, please, Madame Zara," Princess Demetra begged. "Look into my future. Tell me what you see!"

The fortune-teller twirled in a circle.

Demetra and Wink jumped out of the way of her swirling red-and-yellow skirt.

When Zara came to a stop, she held a small glass ball in her hand.

"Where did that come from?" Demetra asked.

"Ask me no questions and I'll tell you no lies," Madame Zara replied.

The fortune-teller held up the glass ball for all to see. It was a snow globe. Inside the glass was a sparkling white palace. A beautiful ice rink stretched in front of it. Several tiny figures skated on the ice.

"That looks like the White Winterland," Demetra gasped.

Madame Zara leaned her face close to Demetra. "It *is* the White Winterland," she whispered.

Demetra stared at the glass ball. "How wonderful!"

Madame Zara nodded. "With this ball I see and hear the future. I know everything that will happen in the White Winterland."

She held the ball close to Demetra's ear. The princess heard a tiny voice say, "I hope the princess invites me to the Diamond Ball. Everyone who is anyone will be there."

Demetra's eyes widened. "That's my friend Wintergreen. I told her that I would like to have a fancy dance at the Diamond Palace someday."

Zara smiled. "It appears your wish will come true."

Demetra shook her head. "That's amazing."

"Would you like to know more?" Madame Zara waved the ball in front of Demetra's face.

"Yes!" Demetra whispered.

"No!" Wink shouted. "You don't want to know the future."

Demetra put her hands on her hips. "I do, too."

"Would you like to own this magic ball?" Madame Zara whispered in Demetra's ear.

Demetra nodded excitedly. "Oh, yes. My own crystal ball."

Wink shook his head. "Bad idea. Very bad idea."

"What do *you* know?" Demetra snapped. "You're just a failed wizard."

For a moment Wink looked hurt. Then he shrugged. "It doesn't take a wizard to know you should never take anything from a Whirligan. They cannot be trusted."

Madame Zara smiled sweetly. "The princess wouldn't be taking anything from me. I ask only for a trade. I'll give her the globe if she gives me something of value."

The Diamond Princess twisted her braid around one finger and tried to think. All she had with her was her crystal sleigh. And she needed that to get home.

Demetra looked up at the fortune-teller. "I'm sorry, but I don't really have anything that I can trade."

"I'm not asking for much," Madame Zara said. "Only a small token."

The fortune-teller cupped one hand around her mouth. She whispered words that only Demetra could hear.

"Don't listen to her," Wink warned. "Please, Princess. You don't know me, but you can trust me. Honest."

The Whirligans who had thrown Wink onto the stage suddenly leaped out of the painted wagon. They tried to grab his arms but the young wizard was too quick for them.

The boy hopped onto a box near the edge of the stage. He pulled a small golden wand out of his knapsack and pointed it at the two men.

"Come any closer, and I'll turn you into little birds!" Wink cried.

Madame Zara burst out laughing. "You can't do it. You don't have the power!"

Wink swallowed hard. "I do, too. Just watch me."

The wizard waved the wand in a circle in front of him and chanted:

"Birds of a feather, take to the sky.
Whirligans, change with a blink of my eye."

Nothing happened.

Wink turned beet-red. He looked at Princess Demetra and shrugged. "I can never remember the exact words. I should have said, *'Fly, you birdies, get off this stage.'* That would have put those two in a cage."

A cloud of blue smoke suddenly filled the air. Demetra heard Wink say, "What the . . . ?"

In a flash, he was gone.

The Beautiful Glass Ball

 The Diamond Princess looked out at the crowd. Wink the Wizard was nowhere to be found.

"The coward ran away," Madame Zara said, holding the ball in front of Demetra. "Forget about him."

Demetra did forget about Wink. She could only stare at the beautiful glass ball.

"Please let me have the magic ball," the

princess said to Madame Zara. "I'll give you whatever you want."

The fortune-teller pulled a tiny pair of scissors from inside her sleeve. She reached for Demetra's beautiful, long brown hair.

Snip!

Madame Zara clipped a tiny lock of hair from the end of Demetra's braid.

"That's it?" Demetra asked.

The fortune-teller tucked the hair into a black velvet bag. "That's it. The magic ball is yours."

The princess couldn't wait to show the beautiful glass ball to Finley, who was waiting in the sleigh.

"Look, Finley!" she cried as she hopped in beside the fox. She showed him her treasure. "Isn't this beautiful?"

"Very beautiful," Finley said, giving Rolf the signal to drive on. "What is it?"

Princess Demetra set the beautiful glass ball on her lap. It sparkled in the bright afternoon sun. "This is a magical globe. It will show me the future."

Demetra expected Finley to be happy for her. But he was just like Wink.

"I don't like the sound of that," Finley muttered. "No one should ever see the future. It's too dangerous. Maybe you should give that thing back."

"No!" The princess wrapped her arms around her new treasure. "I won't. It's mine. I traded the Whirligan for it, fair and square."

Finley sighed. "There are good Whirligans and bad Whirligans. Are you sure Madame Zara is a good one?"

"Of course I'm sure," Princess Demetra replied. "She was very sweet to me. She guessed who I was, and she gave me this beautiful gift."

As the sleigh reached the top of the hill, the Diamond Princess turned to wave good-bye to Madame Zara and the Whirligans. But the dancers and musicians were gone. So was the colorful painted wagon.

In its place sat a drab cart. Several figures in black cloaks huddled next to it.

Demetra sat up to get a better look at them. But the sleigh slipped over the hill and the cart disappeared from sight.

"That's strange," she murmured.

"What is, my lady?" Finley asked.

"Oh, nothing," Demetra said, leaning back in her seat. She wasn't sure what she'd seen. "Maybe it was just a trick of the light. Let's go home."

Rolf the reindeer pulled the sleigh along the border of the White Winterland. As they drove, Demetra carefully held the magical ball in her lap.

When they came to the road leading to Princess Demetra's palace, the reindeer stumbled to a stop.

"What's the matter, Rolf?" Finley asked.

The reindeer looked confused. "I thought this was the road to the Diamond Palace. But it can't be."

"Why not?" Demetra asked.

"Look." Rolf pawed at the ground.

It used to be covered in a smooth carpet of snow. Now it was a muddy mess.

"The snow is gone from the fir trees." Rolf nodded to the woods. The trees were completely green. Water dripped off their branches onto the ground.

Demetra stood up. This was her kingdom, all right. And this was definitely her royal road. But something was terribly wrong.

"My snow!" the princess gasped. "It's melting!"

White Winterland Is Melting!

"Look at Sparkle Mountain!" Finley the fox pointed at the big mountain in the distance.

Its peak used to glitter with white snow. Now it was brown.

"This is a complete disaster!" Demetra cried.

"How could this happen?" Finley whispered.

"I'm not sure," Demetra murmured.

"We need to get to the Diamond Palace and find out. Rolf! Please, let's hurry!"

The reindeer ducked his head and tried to drag the sleigh through the deep mud. "I can't move it!" he gasped.

Demetra and Finley jumped out to lighten the load. But that didn't help.

"It's no use," Rolf huffed. "We're stuck! The runners of the sleigh are buried in the mud."

The Diamond Princess turned in a circle. Everywhere she looked, the snow was melting. Soon her beautiful White Winterland would be one big mud puddle.

"I don't know what's the matter," she said to Finley. "But I think we need help. Big help."

"Your parents?" Finley asked. "Queen Jemma and King Regal?"

The Diamond Princess shook her head. "Bigger than that. We need Gallivant."

Just mentioning the great wizard's name made Finley snap to attention. "I'll leave at once."

"You can't go on foot. Ride on Rolf's back." Demetra unharnessed the reindeer. "It'll be much quicker. I'll hike back to the palace."

Finley saluted, then hopped onto the reindeer's back and patted his neck. "Are you ready, friend?"

Rolf took a deep breath. "Let's go."

With a bound, the reindeer leaped across the muddy road into the field. He and Finley were out of sight in no time.

Princess Demetra picked up the glass ball without looking at it. She draped the hem of her long cape over one arm and followed the muddy road, trying not to step in too many puddles.

She came upon a herd of mountain goats standing miserably under a tree. "Princess, it's so hot!" the oldest goat panted. "What is happening to White Winterland?"

"I don't know," Demetra called back. "But I'm going to do my best to find out."

Demetra climbed Alpine Ridge to catch a glimpse of the Diamond Palace.

At the top of the ridge, the princess was startled to find a huge birdcage hanging from a tree. It was on the edge of the cliff.

Inside was a boy in a green tunic and brown tights. A small green frog sat next to him.

"Wink?" Demetra gasped. "Is that you?"

The boy clutched the bars of the cage. "Yes, it's me. Help! The cage is locked."

Demetra looked around for something to break the lock.

"Don't worry, Wink!" the princess called. "I'll get you out of there!"

Demetra hurled three huge rocks at the lock on the birdcage. She had to be careful not to hit Wink or Trumpet, the frog. The first rock chipped one corner of the lock. The second cracked the lock in two. The third rock freed Wink from the cage.

"Thanks!" Wink gasped. He and Trumpet hopped out of the cage and stepped quickly away from the edge of the cliff. "I could have never gotten out of that cage by myself!"

Demetra watched as the young wizard checked to make sure his frog, Trumpet, was all right. Then he tried to straighten his wand.

"How did this happen?" the princess asked.

Wink shook his head. "I'm not sure. My spell turned on me. Madame Zara must have done something. She has very strong magic."

Hearing the fortune-teller's name, Demetra remembered the magic ball. She had set it down when she saw the trouble Wink was in.

Wink and Demetra found the magic ball on top of a flat gray rock. But it didn't look at all like it had before.

"Look! The White Winterland inside the glass has melted, too," Demetra groaned. "It looks exactly like the White Winterland outside the ball."

Wink scratched his chin. "I wonder if

this ball is the cause of your problem."

Demetra felt the glass. It was very warm. "Do you think the sun melted the snow inside the ball, and that made the snow melt in the White Winterland?"

"It's possible." Wink looked at the princess. "You didn't do anything foolish, did you? Like make a wish?"

"Of course not," Demetra replied. "At least, not while I was holding the magic ball."

"Did you make a wish before that?" Wink asked.

Demetra's eyes were suddenly two huge circles of blue. "Yes, I did."

"What was your wish?" Wink asked.

"I wished that the White Winterland was no longer white," Demetra said with a groan. "I wanted to be able to swim and pick flowers in the grass."

The two of them stared at the snowy mountains melting inside the glass ball.

"Oh, Wink," Demetra whispered. "My wish came true. This magic ball is melting all the snow in the White Winterland."

5

Higglety-Pigglety-*Poof*!

 "I can make it snow again," Wink announced.

"You?" Demetra said. "How?"

Wink shrugged. "I'll just wave my wand."

"Maybe you shouldn't." Demetra pointed to the frog, who was sitting on the ground. "Look what happened to your poor dog, Trumpet."

Trumpet wiggled his bottom and sat up on his hind legs. "Woof!"

Demetra shook her head. "I don't want that to happen to my kingdom."

Wink threw his arms in the air. "How hard can it be to make this tiny ball cold again? Let me try it!"

"Okay," Demetra said finally. "But be careful."

"Don't worry!" Wink replied. He swung his wand in big circles above his head.

"Something soft and something white.
Fill the sky with this tonight."

Poof!

Instantly the sky was full of soft white feathers.

"That's not snow!" Demetra cried, as they floated onto her cheeks and eyelashes. "It looks like a pillow exploded."

"Oh, dear," Wink muttered. "How did that spell go? I studied the first part but I forgot about the second part."

"Aaaah-*CHOO!*" Demetra sneezed loudly.

"Baaaah-*ROO!*" Trumpet sneezed, too. The feathers poured out of the sky. They stuck to everything — the trees, the rocks, and the Diamond Princess.

The princess spit feathers out of her mouth. "Ick!"

Wink swatted at the feathers with his wand. "I'll try it again."

Before Demetra could stop him, he chanted:

"Higglety-pigglety, feathers off trees,
Put White Winterland in a deep freeze!"

The feathers vanished.

Princess Demetra looked at the glass globe. She watched in horror as the Diamond Palace, Sparkle Mountain, and all of her people were frozen in a great big block of ice!

Run from the Ice!

 "Look at my palace. And look at my people," Demetra cried. "They're frozen solid. What did you do?"

"I don't think *I* did anything," Wink said, shaking his head. "It's that glass ball. How could it have such strong magic?"

Princess Demetra peered over the cliff's edge. A band of white frost slowly spread from the Diamond Palace out across the White Winterland.

"I don't know," she murmured. "But if we don't get out of here, we'll be frozen like everyone else."

"You're right." Wink picked up his knapsack and frog, Trumpet. "We'd better run!"

Princess Demetra grabbed the frozen ball and ran beside Wink. They raced back toward the border.

"What did you give Madame Zara?" Wink huffed as the crystal sleigh came into view. Beyond the sleigh lay the edge of the Mysterious Forest.

"Nothing much," Demetra replied. "Only a small lock of my hair."

"What!" Wink stumbled to a halt. "You gave her your hair?"

The Diamond Princess nodded. "What's wrong with that?"

"This is *terrible!*" he wailed. "Now Madame Zara has the power to control your life."

Demetra was really worried. "How can she do that?"

"You gave her a part of you." Wink pointed to the snow globe. "You thought that glass ball could show you the future. But it is Madame Zara who is deciding the future."

"You mean Madame Zara made the snow melt?" Demetra gasped. "And Madame Zara put my kingdom in a deep freeze?"

Wink groaned. "Yes. But my bad spells didn't help."

The princess stared at the tiny glass

ball, and her frozen palace inside. "This is all my fault," she whispered. "If I hadn't been in such a hurry to see the future, I would have noticed what was happening in the present."

"You couldn't have known." Wink patted the princess on the shoulder. "Don't be too hard on yourself."

"I have to be," Demetra snapped. "I am the Diamond Princess. I have to look after my people. I got us into this mess. Now it's up to me to get us out of it."

"But how?" the wizard asked.

Demetra took a deep breath. "I have to get my lock of hair back."

"You're right," Wink agreed. "But we'll have to move fast. Madame Zara and her Whirligans are probably deep in the Mysterious Forest by now."

Demetra climbed into her crystal

sleigh. It was still stuck in the mud.

"I wish this sleigh was a wagon with wheels," she sighed. "And we had a horse to pull it. Then we'd have a chance of finding Zara."

"That's easy." Wink shoved back his sleeves. "That was one of our beginner spells. I'm pretty sure I remember it."

Before Demetra could stop him, Wink waved his wand.

Plink!

The beautiful crystal sleigh was gone. In its place stood an old wooden cart. Trumpet was pulling the cart. But Trumpet was no longer a frog or a dog. He was a pig!

"Trumpet!" Wink cried. "What have I done to you now?"

Trumpet turned his snout to look at them and woofed loudly.

A chill froze the air. Princess Demetra

looked behind her. The frost was creeping up the road.

She picked up the reins and shouted, "Wink, don't worry about Trumpet. The frost is almost here. Jump into the cart!"

Wink leaped into the cart, and Trumpet the barking pig pulled the cart to the border of Demetra's land.

The trio left the frozen White Winterland just in time.

When they entered the Mysterious Forest, everything changed. The air smelled like rotting leaves. It was dark and very scary. Black vines hung from the twisted tree limbs.

Demetra pulled back on Trumpet's reins. She was certain she heard whispers in the shadows.

"I don't like it here," she murmured. "We should leave."

"No!" Wink insisted. "We have to search the Mysterious Forest. I'm sure Madame Zara is here."

Demetra pulled her white cape tight around her. "I just wish I knew where."

Wink raised his wand. "I'll use my magic and find out."

Demetra had seen what happened when Wink waved his wand. She didn't want to risk being turned into a frog or a pig and being trapped in the dark woods. She grabbed his arm.

"Excuse me, Wink," she said. "I think it's time for me to use *my* magic."

"You have magic?" Wink asked in surprise.

Demetra felt for the beautiful jeweled mirror that hung from the waist of her dress. It gave her the power to see people and things in other places.

"Gallivant gave me this when I was crowned the Diamond Princess," she said.

Wink was impressed. "If the great Wizard Gallivant gave that to you, it must have very good magic indeed."

Demetra smiled and raised her magic mirror:

"Oh, magic mirror, so bright and true,
Where are the Whirligans, and Zara, too?"

The glass in the mirror turned into a reflecting pool. Demetra and Wink saw a figure in a crowded marketplace. It was Madame Zara, standing with the Whirligans by her wagon.

"That must be the Bizarre Bazaar," Wink cried. "It lies in the Borderlands, at the edge of the Mysterious Forest."

"I've heard stories about it," Demetra murmured.

"It's an amazing place," Wink replied. "You can buy or sell anything there."

"What would Madame Zara be selling?" Demetra asked.

She was answered by the picture in the mirror. The fortune-teller held up a small black velvet bag.

"That's the bag with my lock of hair in it!" Demetra gasped.

"Oh, dear," Wink muttered. "It looks like that evil Madame Zara is going to sell your hair." He pointed behind the wagon. "To those creatures in black capes. I wonder who they are."

Demetra felt a chill go up her spine. She knew very well who those creatures were. Her mother and father had warned her about them her entire life.

"Darklings!" she whispered. "Madame Zara is selling my hair to the Darklings!"

The Bizarre Bazaar

 The Darklings worked for the evil Lord Bleak. He was a very bad man who once ruled the Jewel Kingdom. Those terrible days were called the Dark Times.

When Lord Bleak was defeated by King Regal and Queen Jemma, he was sent far away across the Black Sea. But every now and then he sent his Darklings back into the Jewel Kingdom to cause trouble.

"Wink, I'm afraid," Demetra confessed as Trumpet pulled the cart toward the Bizarre Bazaar. "When I was growing up, my mother told us stories of the Darklings. They used to be beautiful. But the evil inside them warped their features. Now they are as ugly outside as they are inside."

"Have you ever seen their faces?" Wink asked.

"No. But my sister Roxanne has." Demetra shuddered. "She said they have pointy teeth and black holes for eyes. Their skin is covered in scars."

Wink made a face. "Let's try to avoid those fellows."

The princess nodded. "I'm with you."

The Bizarre Bazaar was a clearing on the edge of the Mysterious Forest. The marketplace was filled with lots of colored wagons, gold-and-black-striped tents, and flags of many lands.

Demetra steered the cart behind a patchwork tent. "Stay," Wink whispered to Trumpet, who woofed in reply. Then he and Demetra peeked around the side of the tent.

"My word!" Demetra gasped. "I've never seen so many different creatures in one place. Not since my coronation, when I was crowned a Jewel Princess."

Green-haired Nymphs from Blue Lake chatted with one-eyed Giants from the Borderlands. Stout Dwarfs from the Red Mountains joked with the furry, long-armed Shinnybins of the Greenwood.

The tables in the market stalls were heaped high with beautiful jewels and clothing. Music filled the air. And everyone talked at once.

The Diamond Princess and Wink were careful to keep out of sight of the crowd. They tiptoed to the next tent to get a closer look.

"Isn't that Clove the Craghopper?" Demetra pointed at a goatlike creature. "She cooks at the Ruby Palace. I'll bet she's buying spices for my sister Roxanne."

Clove handed a pointy-eared Elf several coins, then moved on.

"That wagon Clove just passed," Wink whispered excitedly. "That's Madame Zara's wagon."

Demetra's eyes widened. "You're right. I recognize the gold stars and moons on the —"

"There she is now!" Wink cut in.

Madame Zara stepped down from her wagon and dove into the crowd. She wore a flowing gold cape that matched her turban. Her eyes were fixed on a black wagon at the other side of the bazaar.

"The Darklings' wagon," Demetra hissed. "Do you see it?"

"I see it, Princess," Wink replied. "And I don't like it."

As Madame Zara approached the black wagon, a hooded figure stepped out from its shadow and came to meet her.

"Wink!" Demetra cried. "She's going to sell my hair. Stop her!"

"How?" Wink asked as the princess pulled him after her through the bazaar.

"Use your magic!" Demetra ordered. She dug in the knapsack on his shoulder. "Here's your wand."

Wink's hand was shaking when he took it. "I can't do it, Princess. I'm a failure. I've never had a spell work. Ever."

"That's because you didn't think it all

the way through," Demetra said, never taking her eyes off Madame Zara as she led them through the crowd. "You're just like me."

Wink was confused. "Have you done spells before?"

"Of course not. But I gave Madame Zara my lock of hair and took that glass ball without really thinking about what might happen."

Wink gulped. "And I wanted to cast my spells without going through all the steps to get them right."

"Exactly."

Demetra had come to the wagon nearest the Darklings. She ducked behind the wagon wheel, pulling Wink down beside her.

"But I'm afraid," Wink confessed. "Lots of things could really go wrong."

Demetra grabbed the little wizard by the shoulders and looked him straight in the eye. "I'm scared, too. But I know you can do this, Wink. I believe in you."

Wink smiled weakly. "Thanks."

"Now take a deep breath," Demetra instructed. "And close your eyes."

Wink did as he was told.

"I want you to use your magic to take that purse away from Madame Zara," Demetra whispered. "Think through every step of the spell that you'll need to do that."

Wink kept his eyes shut, and nodded.

As he thought, Demetra peered around the wagon wheel.

Madame Zara and the Darkling were smiling! Demetra watched as Madame Zara reached inside her cape and pulled out the tiny black velvet bag with Demetra's hair in it.

The princess clutched Wink's arm. "Wink? I hope you're done thinking. Because it's now or never. Which will it be?"

"Now!" Wink's eyes popped open and he sprang out from behind the wagon. "Zara! Look at me!"

Wink's booming voice made the fortune-teller spin around in fear. When she saw who it was, her eyes narrowed. "You! What are you doing here?"

"Ask me no questions and I'll tell you no lies!" Wink replied.

Then he raised both hands above his head. One held the golden wand.

"Send me the bag with the princess's hair.
Fly away, spirits, take to the air!"

The black velvet bag shot out of Madame Zara's hand.

"What?" Zara cried. "Come back!"

The velvet bag whizzed like an arrow over the Darklings' heads. It landed in Wink's empty hand.

"Bull's-eye!" Wink whispered.

"You did it!" Demetra cheered, leaping up beside him.

The young wizard bowed formally to the princess, and handed her the bag. "I believe this belongs to you, Princess Demetra."

"That was incredible!" Demetra gushed. "You sounded so powerful. Just like a real wizard."

Wink's grin stretched from ear to ear. But his smile suddenly faded. "I'd love to hear more about it, Princess, but we seem to have a small problem."

Wink pointed behind Demetra. Madame Zara and three of the Darklings were coming toward them. And they looked very angry.

"What should we do?" Demetra cried. "There's nowhere to run."

Wink didn't answer. His eyes were shut tight.

Madame Zara and the Darklings grew closer.

Demetra backed up against a wagon. "Wink? Um, Wink! What are you doing?"

"I'm thinking." Wink raised his wand. He murmered a few strange words.

The first Darkling reached for Demetra with a long bony hand. The princess opened her mouth to scream.

Wink waved his wand and —

Poof!

The Bizarre Bazaar was gone.

Wink the Magnificent

Demetra and Wink found themselves sitting on a sparkling white snowbank. Tall evergreens surrounded them. In the distance they could just see a snow-capped mountain.

"Where are we?" Wink asked as he tried to stand up.

Princess Demetra knew very well where they were. This was her home.

"We're in the White Winterland," she whispered. "And it's the way it should be. Thanks to you."

Wink the Wizard blushed. "If you hadn't helped me to believe in myself, I wouldn't be here."

"And if you hadn't helped me to understand I didn't need a crystal ball to change the future," Demetra said, "I wouldn't be here."

"Now, if I could just fix Trumpet, everything . . ." Wink's voice trailed off as he realized his dog-turned-frog-turned-pig wasn't with them.

"Trumpet?" Wink spun in a circle, looking for the barking pig. "I left him in the Bizarre Bazaar! How could I do such a thing?"

His cries were answered by a loud "Woof!"

A huge brown-and-black hound dog,

with long ears and droopy eyes, galloped out of the woods. He was pulling a crystal sleigh behind him.

"It's Trumpet! He's a dog again!"

While Trumpet licked every inch of Wink's face, Demetra unhitched the sleigh. "My beautiful sleigh is back."

Wink wiped his face with his sleeve. "Do you think it's possible that all the bad spells have been broken?"

"Let me see." The princess felt in the pocket of her dress for the little snow globe. She had carried it with her through their entire adventure.

"Look, Wink! The White Winterland isn't inside anymore."

Wink hurried to look at the snow globe.

The Diamond Palace was gone. In its place was a tiny cottage with carved

wooden shutters and a stone chimney.

"That cottage looks familiar," Wink said. "It belongs to someone I know."

The cottage door opened and a man with long white hair and an even longer white beard stepped onto the front step.

"Gallivant!" Demetra and Wink gasped together.

The wizard looked up at them and smiled. "Greetings!"

"Wh-wh-what are you doing in there?" Wink stammered. It was clear from the look on his face that Wink was afraid his spell had gone wrong. Had he somehow imprisoned the great wizard in the snow globe?

"Don't panic, lad," Gallivant said with a chuckle. "Everything is all right. I've come to congratulate you both on a job well done. It wasn't easy to face Madame Zara."

The Diamond Princess and the young

wizard both blushed. "Thank you," they replied.

"Demetra, you have your kingdom back the way it was," Gallivant continued. "And Finley and Rolf are on their way home. They should be there any minute."

"That is good news!" Demetra said with a smile.

Gallivant turned to Wink. "And you, lad, have proven yourself to be a real wizard."

"Me!" Wink gasped. "A real, genuine wizard?"

Gallivant arched one eyebrow. "Let's just call you a real, genuine wizard-in-training. Report back here first thing tomorrow morning, and we'll continue your lessons."

"Yes, sir!" Wink said with a salute. "I'll be there."

"Good." Gallivant nodded to Princess Demetra, then disappeared inside his cottage.

Demetra grinned at Wink. "A real, genuine wizard. This calls for a celebration. A fancy dance. Just like Wintergreen wanted." She clapped her hands together. "That's the gift I'll give my people. A Diamond Ball."

"It sounds wonderful," Wink said.

"It will be," Demetra cried. "We'll have music and a feast, with lots of cakes and cookies."

"One cake coming right up!" Wink said, waving his wand wildly in the air.

A cake exploded out of the ground and shot high in the air. Trumpet caught it in his mouth and swallowed it whole.

"Oops," Wink said in a tiny voice. "I forgot to think. Let me try again."

"I have a better idea," Demetra said,

taking the wand and putting it safely away in Wink's knapsack. "When Finley and Rolf return, we'll all go back to the Diamond Palace. There we can whip up a batch of snowdrop cookies the old-fashioned way."

"What's the old-fashioned way?" Wink asked.

"We'll bake them," Demetra replied with a grin.

"That sounds good to me," Wink said.

"What do you think, Trumpet?" Demetra asked.

For the first time Demetra understood how Trumpet got his name. The hound dog tilted back his snout and let out the loudest, happiest howl she had ever heard.

"Bar-*roooooooooo!*"

About the Authors

JAHNNA N. MALCOLM stands for Jahnna "and" Malcolm. Jahnna Beecham and Malcolm Hillgartner are married and write together. They have written over seventy books for kids. Jahnna N. Malcolm have written about ballerinas, horses, ghosts, singing cowgirls, and green slime.

Before Jahnna and Malcolm wrote books, they were actors. They met on the stage where Malcolm was playing a prince. And they were married on the stage where Jahnna was playing a princess.

Now they have their own little prince and princess: Dash and Skye. They all live in Ashland, Oregon, with their big red dog, Ruby, and their fluffy little white dog, Clarence.